W9-BLS-055

TIME FOR BED
LITTLE KIWI

PUFFIN BOOKS

Written and illustrated by
Bob Darroch

Mother Kiwi called Little Kiwi to come home.

It's time for bed.

But where is Little Kiwi?

Is he in the fern bush?

Is he in the high branches of the big tree?

Where can Little Kiwi be?

Is he in the hollow log?

Where are you Little Kiwi?

Is he in the cave behind
the waterfall?

Come home Little Kiwi!

Is he high in the berry tree?

It's bedtime Little Kiwi!

Is he at the beach?

Time to come home Little Kiwi!

Is he under the
fallen tree?

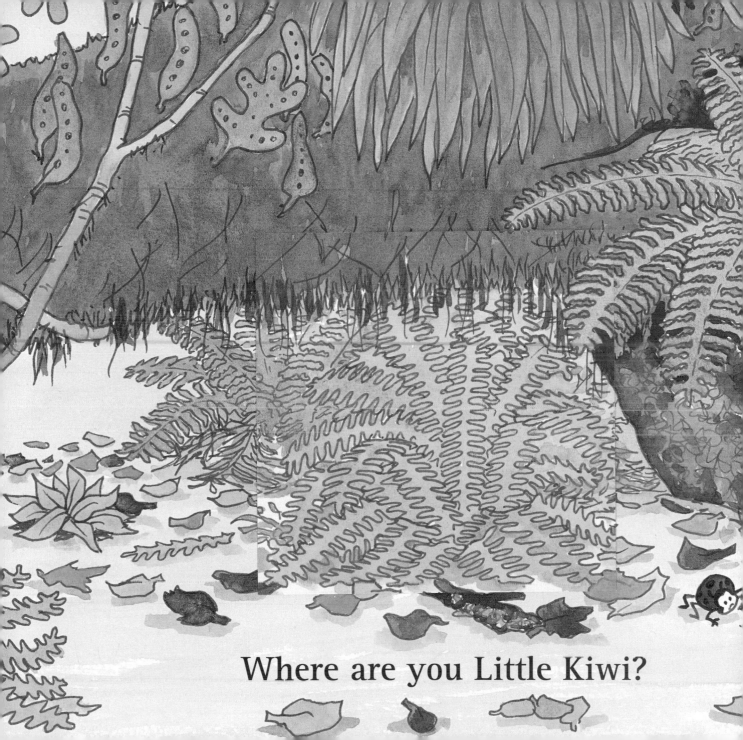

Where are you Little Kiwi?

Is he in the flax bushes?

Where can Little Kiwi be?

Is he in the wetland?

Where is Little Kiwi?

Is he in the ti-tree bushes?

It's time to come home, Little Kiwi.

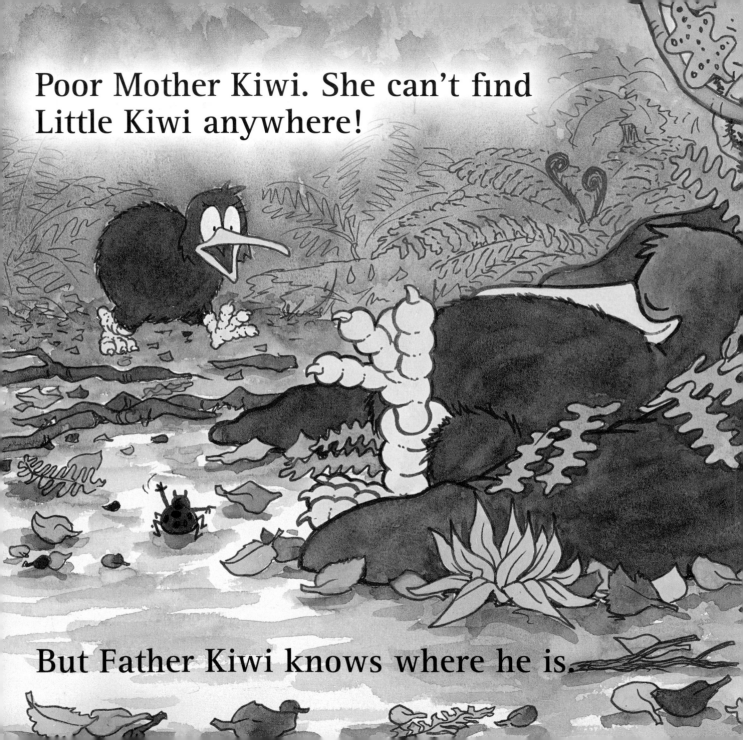

Poor Mother Kiwi. She can't find
Little Kiwi anywhere!

But Father Kiwi knows where he is.

Little Kiwi is in his bed – fast asleep.

Little Kiwi is tired but happy after a
fun-filled night playing with all his friends.

Sleep tight Little Kiwi!